W9-BLG-500

This First Thanksgiving Day

A COUNTING STORY

by Laura Krauss Melmed

illustrated by Mark Buehner

■ HARPERCOLLINSPUBLISHERS

I dressed in linen,
sitting in a tree,
dreaming of the tall, strong ship
on which he crossed the sea.

2 dressed in deerskin,
gathering nuts below,
giggling as they tiptoe by,
too shy to say hello.

3 in the garden,
pulling up some roots—
turnips for the pottage pot
and parsnips for the soup.

4 helping Father
catch fish in the bay—
some to dry for wintertime
and some to eat today.

5 in the forest,
searching as they roam—
finding sticks to light the fire
that keeps them warm at home.

6 stepping softly
with small bows in hand,
following a rabbit's tracks
across a patch of sand.

7 fetching water
run with pails to fill,
then walk home with careful steps
so not a drop will spill.

8 on the sandbar,
working in a crew—

digging for some tasty clams
to make a steaming stew.

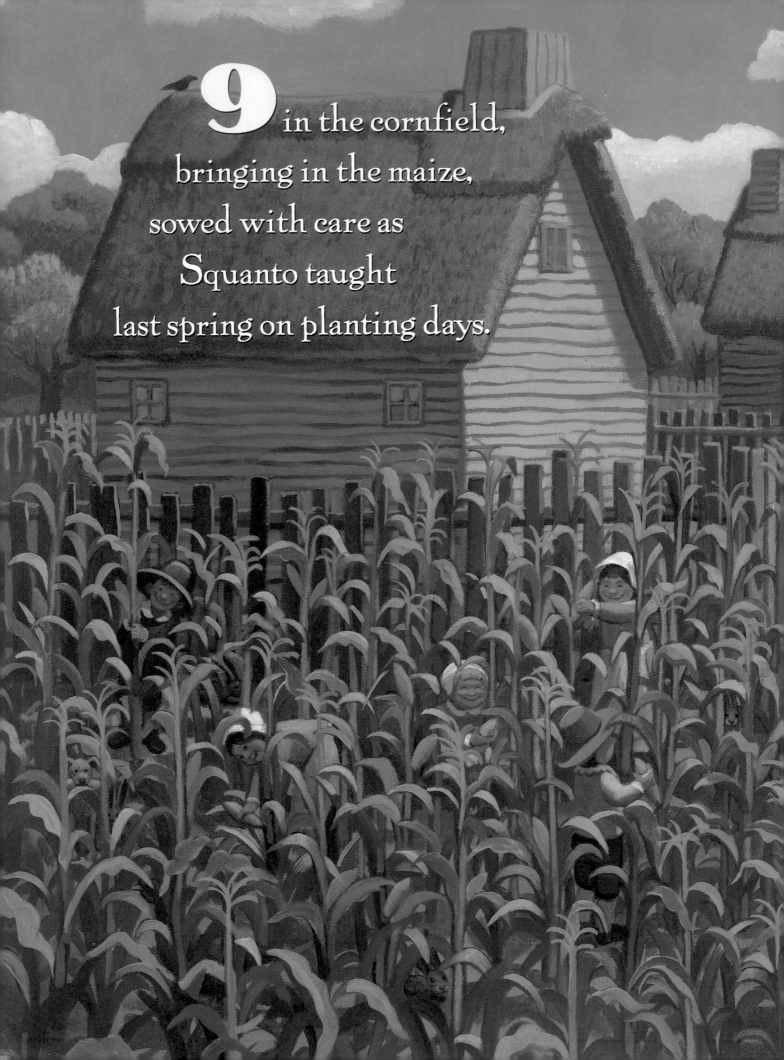

9 in the cornfield,
bringing in the maize,
sowed with care as
Squanto taught
last spring on planting days.

10 making baskets
by the fire's glow,
weaving slender cattail reeds
while singing soft and low.

rejoicing
in the autumn sun—
laughing, shouting, playing tag,
their chores at last all done.

12 tables groaning
beneath a harvest spread—
Wampanoag and Pilgrim friends
together will break bread.

Joined under one sky
with one prayer to say—
a prayer of thanks for all they have
this first Thanksgiving Day.

In memory of my grandmothers, Sadie Krauss and Lillian Engel,
who voyaged to the New World in their time
—L.K.M.

To Sam, Laura, and Jake, my littlest beans
—M.B.

This First Thanksgiving Day
Text copyright © 2001 by Laura Krauss Melmed
Illustrations copyright © 2001 by Mark Buehner
Manufactured in China. All rights reserved.
www.harperchildrens.com

Library of Congress Cataloging-in-Publication Data
Melmed, Laura Krauss.
This first Thanksgiving day / by Laura Krauss Melmed ; illustrated by Mark Buehner.
p.   cm.
Summary: Twelve short poems that combine counting with the story of the first Thanksgiving.
ISBN 0-688-14554-X — ISBN 0-688-14555-8 (lib. bdg.) — ISBN 0-06-054184-9 (pbk.)
1. Thanksgiving Day—Juvenile poetry.   2. Children's poetry, American.
[1. Thanksgiving Day—Poetry.   2. American poetry.   3. Counting.]   I. Buehner, Mark, ill.   II. Title.
PS3563.E4429 A12   2001   811'.54—dc20   [E] 96-14215

Typography by Al Cetta

❖